The Journal of Brock Adair

1771 – 1844
The Resident Detective of Ballymena

– NED BYRNE –

Cover Illustration by
Erinn Byrne

FASTPRINT PUBLISHING
PETERBOROUGH, ENGLAND

THE JOURNAL OF BROCK ADAIR
Copyright © Ned Byrne 2010

All rights reserved.

No part of this book may be reproduced in any form by photocopying or any electronic or mechanical means, including information storage or retrieval systems, without permission in writing from both the copyright owner and the publisher of the book.

ISBN 978-184426-838-2

First published 2010 by
FASTPRINT PUBLISHING
Peterborough, England.

Printed in England by
www.printondemand-worldwide.com

In memory of Carol

The Journal of Brock Adair

In 2006 a bundle of hand written pages were discovered buried in a garden in the outskirts of Cullybackey near Ballymena, County Antrim. They had been sealed in sacking and placed in a wooden box which had been covered in what appeared to be bitumen. The contents revealed the journal of one Brock Adair outlining his investigations into crime in the Antrim area and in particular the area of Ballymena in the eighteenth and nineteenth century. This had been a period of turbulence for that community, indeed for Ireland. This investigator had not been heard of in modern times, yet within these entries are outlined his successes in bringing perpetrators to justice. These included one Thomas Archer a notorious criminal of the late 1700's, who was hanged in Ballymena at the moat. These notes were tied neatly in black ribbon and were accompanied by a large envelope. Inside the envelope was discovered handwritten letters by a Charles Kinhilt a solicitor from the Cullybackey area. These are the words this gentleman penned: -

Ned Byrne

Sir/Madam

It is the year 1844 my name is Charles Kinhilt, I am a lawyer from Cullybackey and I practice my profession in the province of Ulster and I commit to paper the following information. My dear friend Brock Adair investigator of this county, this town of Ballymena, has passed away, in this year of 1844 on the fifth of May. He has been laid to rest on private ground in the Brocklamont area of Ballymena by special permission from the Authorities.

Dear reader, I would like to outline some details of my friend's life and times for the future, so that those of this area and of the surrounding villages will know the works of this fine man. Brock Adair was a gentleman, a fine investigator, and an astute observer of people and places. He was also a man who liked his privacy, he being humble and unassuming. Were it not for the professional investigations of my dear friend Brock many a felon would still be outstanding in this district, causing havoc and hurt. Brock assisted the authorities with many an investigation, some serious, some amusing. I have attached herewith a number of investigations of Brock Adair and perhaps it's true to say that Brock would not want these notes, these investigations to be made public. I feel however, that sometime in the future it would be pertinent, indeed proper, for such investigations to be made public. I now outline the life and times of my very dear friend Brock Adair.

In the year of 1771 in the month of July, a warm month indeed, Brock was found abandoned on private land in the Brocklamont area of Ballymena. He was found well wrapped near the highway. It appeared that he was a newborn infant perhaps just hours old. The owner of said land Mrs Elizabeth Adair had been walking and discovered the child. She and her husband Bruce were wealthy, kindly folk and it was their wish having failed to trace the mother of this infant that they would raise the child as theirs. He was given the name Brock after the area of Ballymena in which he was found. This area was known for its numerous badger setts. I have learned of late that the word Brock means badger in Irish.

He had a good upbringing studying law at Trinity College in Dublin. He always wanted to return to Ballymena the place of his birth, and did so in 1796 during the summer. I had the privilege of meeting Brock at Trinity College Dublin during the year 1794. Our friendship grew as did our circle of friends, he was at ease with all walks of society and I noticed early on that if you treated him with respect he reciprocated. He had no airs or graces. It was on an occasion in a tavern not far from Kells that Brock mentioned to me his deep desire to do something about the ever increasing lawlessness which without doubt was affecting the town he loved. He felt he could help out the authorities in their endeavour to bring some form of peace and security to the region.

It was indeed in the year 1796 that Brock was to get an opportunity to assist the authorities and that is where his first case occurred. The murder of one Florence McSorley in Meeting House Lane, Ballymena, on a dark evening in October 1796. The account of this investigation is part of Mr Adair's journals which are attached.

It should be noted too that Brock married a lass called Veronica Jessop from Ahoghill; she bore him a son Theobald, who to this day continues the work that his father started. As I pen these words he is assisting the newly formed police force with numerous enquiries, not only in the county of Antrim but throughout the length and breadth of Ireland. As I have stated Brock was a fine, good looking man with thick black hair which he retained all his life. Brock never wore headgear; he disliked anything on his hair. He was also in a light hearted way, exact about his height; it was five foot eleven and three quarter inches. He was an accomplished horseman, also one who could shoot a pistol with the finest of accuracy. I feel impelled to mention that Brock hated wearing light coloured garments. Although in his early twenties Brock acquired the reputation of being an accomplished investigator. Captain Dickey of the military in Ballymena certainly held this opinion and it proved to be so as the years went by.

There is dear reader one further account I wish to place on record as being fact. You will know that in 1798 a rebellion in this land occurred. You will know of one of its leaders – Theobald Wolfe Tone. I wish to place on record that Brock met with Wolfe Tone in the outskirts of Ballymena about a year before the rebellion. This meeting was in relation to a number of attacks on females in the town of Wexford. Brock's reputation had spread far and wide and Wolfe Tone requested Brock to investigate these crimes. I can tell you dear reader, that Brock was successful in this matter. I have detailed the Wexford investigation in this journal. You will know also that the rebellion affected Ballymena also, with skirmishes in Bridge Street and Shambles Street. I wish to make clear that Brock took no part in this rebellion.

Attached you will find accounts of some of the investigations that my friend Brock Adair conducted. I have detailed these accounts on the attached papers. These are some of the cases that Brock was involved in and successfully concluded: -

The Murder of Florence McSorley in Meeting House Lane, Ballymena – 1796

Sylvia Ferguson, the missing infant of Cullybackey

The Harryville Burglar

The Wexford Attacks

The Avian Thief of Ahoghill

The Accomplice in Star Bog

The Shambles Street Arsonist

The Highwayman of Ballymarlagh

The Pickpocket at Cullybackey Racecourse

The Robbery of the Provincial Bank of Wellington Street – 1835

An Emotional Reunion at Pennybridge

The Munie Road Highwayman

Torys in the Glens

Abduction of Miss Sylvia Lanyon

An American at Deerfin

These are but some of the enquiries that I have carefully detailed so that you may appreciate the work of this wonderful man. I conclude that I have outlined truthfully as much detail and fact as I possibly can with respect to Brocks investigations. I am confident also that his son Theobald will continue the good works of his father. I feel impelled to mention Veronica his dear wife. She is a fine lady who has been a supportive mother and wife. I feel pity for her at this time, but I also know that pity does not heal the wounds of death. I will continue to be as supportive as I can, having myself lost my wife recently in death. Ballymena has lost a fine citizen, his family a father and husband. I was privileged to know him and have him as a friend and confidante.

Signed Charles Kinhilt.

1 June 1844.

The Murder of Florence McSorley in Meeting House Lane Ballymena – 1796

Ned Byrne

Chapter One

The bitter wind searched the length and breadth of Meeting House Lane, Ballymena, on this dark October evening. Florence McSorley would be a victim of another bitter force. As was her habit, she walked from her elderly mother's house to her home in Shambles Street a short distance away. Only she would not arrive home.

About 9pm on that Thursday evening of late October 1796 her fully clothed, but mortally wounded body was found in a large pool of blood. It was discovered on close examination, that she was stabbed several times on her neck, body and leg. Captain Dickey of the military stationed in Ballymena attended the gruesome scene, and despite years of experience he was appalled by what he saw. Here lay Mrs McSorley, 38 years old, a married woman with two daughters, such an outrageous thing to occur in Ballymena. Captain Dickey dispatched one of his men to inform her husband. Mrs McSorley was well known in the town so identification was not difficult.

There are no details of the family's reaction to such news, suffice to say it would have been harrowing. Captain Dickey knew that the offender or offenders would need to be detained hastily and brought before the courts. Indeed he feared that further attacks would occur, as it had seemed so random. Turning to his soldiers he commanded "Summon Brock Adair! With great haste!"

About 10.30pm Brock Adair attended the scene on Meeting House Lane. He greeted Captain Dickey, and dismounted his black horse Duke. Securing him near the church he then approached the body slowly. Adair was wearing his, by now, trademark black outer coat with high collar, no headwear, and as usual his high black boots were immaculately polished. He had long thick black hair, immaculately groomed. He had no facial hair. It was obvious Adair gave attention to detail, not only in investigations but to his appearance as well. This tall, pensive figure eluded charisma.

"Captain Dickey sir", he looked to Captain Dickey, "I will assist as best I can".

"I know you will Brock, I know".

"Would it be possible for me to have a moment alone with this unfortunate lady and the surroundings?"

"Why of course, of course! Clear the way for Mr Adair, men." Captain Dickey ordered. A large crowd had by now gathered, many openly wept and were astonished that such a despicable crime like this could occur.

Brock stood back from the body, "Are there any witness at all captain?" Captain Dickey shook his head. Brock pondered for a moment. "The lady, Mrs McSorley lived in Shambles Street with her husband and two daughters did she not? How tall is Mr McSorley?"

"I don't know, but I shall determine that for you" Captain Dickey replied.

"Thank you captain, it is of the utmost importance." Brock stopped beside the body observing every detail. "I need my friend Charles Kinhilt in attendance please. I must request that he bring his sketch book. I will meet Charles here at 8 o' clock in the morning. Captain your men are staying at the scene until daylight are they not?"

"Indeed they are Brock, and I will ask my men to summon Mr Kinhilt, rest assured Brock that the scene will remain secured" said Captain Dickey.

The next day Brock attended the scene at 8:00am sharp. He was joined by Charles a short while later.

On seeing the body Charles remarked "such an upsetting thing to occur, what evil thing has done this?"

"I don't know as yet Charles, but we shall do our damndest to find the felon."

"Yes, we must find this perpetrator." Charles said in a strong voice.

"Please draw the scene for me, particularly the marks on the body, and Charles, please include those shavings at the side of the body." Said Brock as he stooped to pick something up and put it in his pocket.

A little while later Kinhilt had finished his sketch of the scene, it was just after 9 o' clock.

Mrs McSorley lay on her back with what appeared to be knife wounds on the side of her body. The poor woman had also been stabbed through the neck, resulting in a long deep scar. Needless to say the scene was thick with blood.

Brock noted that she was a tall woman at least five feet eleven inches.

"Captain Dickey sir, you may wish to reunite the lady with her family and her clergy. I shall report to you in due course."

"Thank you Brock." Captain Dickey turned and went away.

"Charles, shall we ride to O'Neil's Arms in Broughshane? I have some business to conduct there."

"Yes of course. May I ask of what nature the business is concerning Brock?"

"Yes Charles, they have a market every week in Broughshane. Yesterday being Thursday, was there not a market held?"

"Yes I understand so." Charles looked somewhat confused.

"If I am not mistaken Charles, there was a special sale of footwear and repair's being promoted at Broughshane market, was there not?"

"Yes it was very well attended Brock".

The rain and strong wind had ceased as Brock and his friend rode into Broughshane, it being about the hour of 12 noon. They tethered their horses at the rear of O'Neil's tavern and entered. A deep, loud voice shouted, "A surprise indeed, and I might add a delight! Welcome Mr Adair, Mr Kinhilt. I will offer you both a glass of Guinness; I know it's your favourite."

"Thank you" replied Brock. "You sir are one of the most congenial publicans in the area Mr Peacock." Brock said with a smile. "That is only one reason why we call!" The pub was busy and a warm turf fire greeted all who entered.

"May I ask what the nature of your visit is my friend at this unusual time, you don't usually call on this day, or at this time?" asked Mr Peacock.

"Well," replied Brock "Thomas, you have been landlord here for twenty or so years, you know the comings and goings do you not?" questioned Brock.

"Aye, a good landlord knows his premises and even better his customers and after twenty three years as such I believe I can read people." He replied. "I would make a fine detective Mr Adair, don't you think?"

"I agree, don't you Charles?" Brock smiled. Charles nodded.

"Yesterday my friend it was a market day?" Brock asked.

"Yes, and one dedicated mainly to cobblers. A fine trade Brock don't you think? It is nice to have comfortable attire on the feet." Thomas replied.

"Yes when it can be afforded. There were a number of repairer's and cobblers doing trade on the main street?"

"There was Brock, I had a pair repaired myself for a small price."

"What time did the market end?"

"About 4pm, it was dull and cold," said Thomas.

"Why are you so intent on this cobbler's market Brock?" asked Charles.

"It is a particular route I need to take Charles."

"In relation to Mrs McSorley?" asked Charles.

"Yes" replied Brock.

"What is this about Brock?" asked Thomas Peacock.

"It is related to what has occurred in Meeting House Lane some hours ago." Brock outlined the circumstances to Thomas, who upon hearing the details of the victim replied angrily, "this felon needs to be caught and dealt with."

"Within the law of course Thomas" replied Brock, "within the law."

"Thomas, you and I have a mutual acquaintance don't we?" asked Brock.

"Ah yes, Archer's friend John Killane, the petty thief . He's in the other room." Thomas replied.

"Would you excuse me gentlemen, I shall return shortly," said Brock.

About 5 minutes later Brock returned, "Charles, one for the road, you're buying."

"Again" said Charles.

After, they bade Thomas Peacock farewell. As they rode toward Ballymena Charles noted that Brock was quiet and indeed pensive. "What ails you my friend?"

"I will tell you. That poor lady had been brutally stabbed," replied Brock.

"Yes I know that Brock, and it is horrible, but is there something else on your mind?"

"Nothing other my friend than that poor lady, her family, her friends, and the fact that there is a felon of the lowest degree at large in our community. I, we, must get him."

"You say him, how do you know it's a 'him', and indeed if he acted alone?"

"Would you agree that observation at all times is paramount Charles? Even as we ride toward Ballymena we observe things, do we not?"

"Yes of course, the cattle in the field and fellow highway users," said Charles.

"That is correct, but surely we need to observe closer and make it the norm for us?"

"But surely that would drive any man mad, having to retain such detail," retorted Charles.

"No my friend. What, for example, was the last rider heading to Broughshane wearing?"

"Well it was dark clothing, yes he had dark clothing."

"And his mount?" Brock probed further.

"The horse was white," Charles said simply.

"Excellent Charles, a white horse easy to see, dark clothing, good, but it was a lady not a man. In fact it was Miss Sylvia Lanyon from Deerfin on her weekly ride through the countryside. She rides the horse in the manner of a man although she is a lady, she is very eccentric. In my profession I need to pay attention to detail. I must, I do, it is second nature to me. Charles, you have many gifts, the ones I admire greatly are your honesty and reliability. I wish I was as reliable a friend to you as you are to me. But there I go again veering from the subject. Let us continue the conversation once we are in Ballymena. I feel I must retire to home. Can I speak with you before noon tomorrow Charles? Please bring with you the sketch you kindly detailed. We shall meet at the Market House in Ballymena at nine o'clock tomorrow, as I also wish to speak to Captain Dickey."

At the Market House they both rode their separate ways, Brock to his home and Charles to his home in the Crebilly area of Ballymena.

Chapter Two

"Good morning Charles," said Brock as he tied his black horse Duke to the railings outside the Market House in Mill Street.

"I trust it will be a good day Brock," replied Charles.

It was about 9.15 am and already Mill Street, Church Street and Bridge Street were busy with people.

"What" said Brock "is the population of our fine town Charles?"

"Well over a thousand, I'd say perhaps more,"

"Of course we have visitors also from other towns and villages," said Brock.

"Yes of course, where shall we go this morning," asked Charles. "What are your plans?"

"Well my friend, I wish to speak with Captain Dickey at his barracks, then we shall continue with our enquiries in the town."

Both men walked the short distance to Captain Dickey's residence.

"Come in gentlemen, come in and let us get to work," said Captain Dickey as he greeted Brock and Charles.

The three men sat down and Brock asked the Captain if his men had established the height of Mr McSorley, the deceased's husband.

"Yes he is about five feet eleven inches, about the same height as his wife," replied the Captain.

"What is his trade?" asked Charles.

"Mr McSorley is a barber, his first name is Thomas and he trades in Shambles Street near his home," said Captain Dickey.

"Does he have an alibi for yesterday," asked Brock.

"Yes," replied Captain Dickey, "his two daughters, Florence who is fourteen years old and Millie who is twenty years old, no twenty one, a single lady."

"Thank you Captain," said Brock, "I appreciate that the family will have much on their minds at the moment, but I need to speak with them."

"Of course," said Captain Dickey, "you may go now if you wish. Mr McSorley wants to help in any way he can, poor man."

"No time like the present," said Brock, "thank you Captain, we will speak again no doubt."

"Of course Brock, we will indeed," replied Captain Dickey.

Charles and Brock walked down Bridge Street and turned right into Shambles Street. It was busy with people and horses. It was Brock who knocked on the door. He noticed the little house was well presented on the outside.

It was obvious that the family had pride in their appearance. It was also obvious that the occupants were in mourning, the curtains on the small front window were closed.

Brock felt apprehensive as he knocked on the front door. He felt like an intruder, but he thought he must ask questions and try and establish facts and not let emotions obstruct his enquiries.

Mr McSorley opened the door.

"My name sir is Brock Adair, and this if my friend Charles Kinhilt, we are helping Captain Dickey."

"I know," said Mr McSorley, "please come in." Mr McSorley looked tired understandably. It was a modest home, but a tidy one, everything in its right place.

"Please accept our condolences Mr McSorley, how are your daughters," asked Brock.

"They are supporting each other and me. The funeral is tomorrow at the Parish Church in Meeting House Lane at eleven o'clock," said Mr McSorley.

"May I ask you some questions Mr McSorley, they will assist with our enquiries?" asked Brock.

"You will have to excuse me gentlemen, I am not thinking straight, but I want to help you catch these people. They have taken my wife and my daughter's mother." Mr McSorley began to sob.

Brock felt uneasy, he cleared his throat. "Mr McSorley, you are a barber by trade?"

"Yes, some thirty one years. I've been thinking about my work, you see shortly after Florence and I met we exchanged gifts even though we were both of little means.

I really love her, she means everything to me, to the girls. She gave me these barbers clippers on our anniversary twenty years ago." Mr McSorley handed the clippers to Brock. "They are still as good as the day I got them," he said.

Brock attempted to operate the clippers but was unable to do so.

"This is how you work them," said Mr McSorley as he demonstrated how to use them.

"We will detain you no longer, but I would like to speak with your daughters, it is important," said Brock.

"They will be home soon, they are with their grandmother," said Mr McSorley.

"We will return," replied Brock. "Charles and I will do our utmost to bring those responsible to justice. Good bye Mr McSorley, and once again please accept our condolences."

Charles and Brock walked toward Bridge Street.

"Where to now Brock," asked Charles.

"We must attend the scene of the murder, I need to establish something," said Brock.

Both men arrived in Meeting House Lane on foot, it was still a cold but very dry day. Captain Dickey had ordered two of his soldiers to remain at the scene at the request of Brock.

"Good day gentlemen, what have you to report," asked Brock.

"Sir," responded one of the cavalrymen, "many people have been passing, women especially, all very upset."

"Yes that is understandable," said Brock. "Can either of you recall any other detail that you think may help?"

"No sir" replied the cavalrymen.

"Thank you" said Brock, "Captain Dickey says you may return to your quarters. If you do recall anything unusual later, please inform me."

"Yes sir" replied both soldiers as they left the scene.

"Have you got the sketch you made of Mrs McSorley, Charles?"

"Yes, I was very detailed, I hope I did not miss anything."

"I'm sure you didn't Charles," replied Brock.

Brock took the sketch and examined it thoroughly. He paced a few yards to the left, then the right. Brock studied the scene carefully. It was apparent Brock was deep in thought as he paced the scene. He always folded his arms and occasionally placed his finger over his mouth. He was muttering to himself as he observed the scene.

"Charles!" he shouted suddenly, "Mrs McSorley was 5 feet eleven inches, that is correct is it not?"

"Yes" replied Charles, "five feet eleven inches precisely."

"She was right handed," said Brock.

"How do you know?" enquired Charles.

"Well" Brock paused, "well, I'm almost certain she was. I will elaborate later my friend. Let us go to Mr McArthur the cobbler in Church Street. I have a pair of black boots for repair."

Meeting House Lane adjoined Church Street and in no time they were at McArthur's. As they entered Brock said to Charles, "please take note of as much detail as possible, about the shop, the cobbler and so forth."

"Good morning gentlemen, what can I help you with?" asked the cobbler.

"Yes, I would like these boots heeled and soled please," said Brock, "and can you put metal clips on the heels please?"

"Of course sir," said the cobbler, "you keep your boots well polished sir, I will have them ready tomorrow morning."

"Excellent" said Brock, "that is quick, you must have an assistant?"

"No sir, I have been working on my own for years. I used to trade in Ballymoney where I come from, my wife is from Ballymena."

"I shall return tomorrow, thank you" said Brock.

Charles and Brock walked slowly to the Market House on Mill Street to collect their horses. Brock greeted Duke and stroked his mane, "you will be fed soon my friend and watered."

"Charles, what did you note in the cobblers McArthurs?"

Charles scratched his head, "well the man was five feet nine inches, slim, clean shaven, his person and his premises were very tidy."

"Good, I concur," said Brock, "anything else?"

"I can't think," and getting a little agitated Charles said, "I cannot recall much else Brock, I am a lawyer not an investigator."

"Yes and a fine lawyer, but lawyers are investigators also Charles, as I've pointed out many times before."

"What have I missed?" Charles enquired.

"Later my friend, later" said Brock. "It has been a busy day Charles, it is time for tea, for our horses also."

"Yes" said Charles, "we have to speak to Florence and Millie, when shall we meet?"

"What time is it now?" asked Brock.

"About one o'clock" replied Charles.

"Can we meet here about five o'clock, it will not take long?" asked Brock.

"Five o'clock" said Charles.

As Brock rode home he was sad but determined to solve the case. He viewed the scene over and over in his mind. The wounds on the right side of the victim, the large incision on the right side of the neck, the angle of that incision. He recalled also the clenched right hand, the red hair and shorter black hair held within that fist. Mrs McSorley had long nails, she must have marked her attacker he thought. She must have, because there was skin and blood under her nails. Also the very small slithers of leather beside the body. I must pay attention to every detail, it is important.

As he approached his home, a beautiful sight appeared in front of him. It was none other than his beloved Veronica Jessop. He loved her, simple as that he thought, I love her. He raced the final few yards, dismounted and ran to her.

"What a nice surprise" he said as he embraced her.

"Your parents invited me to dine with you this evening" said Veronica.

"Good, no excellent" said Brock.

Greeting his parents he asked what time dinner would be served.

"Seven thirty, precisely, and you better be in attendance my lad" replied his mother.

"Yes mother, I will be" said Brock.

With Duke fed and watered, Brock strolled around the garden with his beloved Veronica.

"I know that you are investigating that ghastly murder Brock, will you catch them?" enquired Veronica.

"I hope so" said Brock.

"The poor lady had a husband and two daughters, poor things" said Veronica

"Yes dear, the world can be a cruel place. Would you allow me to protect and look after you forever?" asked Brock.

"Of course Brock, in fact I demand it" replied Veronica laughingly.

They continued to stroll around the garden, kissing whenever out of sight of the house.

"I must attend Ballymena, but only for half an hour or so" said Brock.

"As long as you are ready for dinner at seven thirty, you wouldn't want to get on the wrong side of your mother, would you?" said Veronica.

"No, not again" replied Brock with a worried look.

He bade farewell to Veronica, promising to return on time.

Brock and Charles met as agreed at five o'clock and made their way to Mr McSorley's home in Shambles Street. The door was opened by Mr McSorley who invited both men inside.

"These are my daughters Florence and Millie" said Mr McSorley by way of introduction.

"Hello" said Brock, he couldn't help but see the girls were pale with grief, he felt deeply moved by their demeanour but was able to control himself. "This is my colleague Mr Charles Kinhilt. Please be assured we will do our best to bring this evil person to justice, yet I realise that this is probably of little comfort to you. Do you have any idea who could do this?"

"No sir, whoever it is, is an evildoer" cried Millie.

"Indeed, indeed" Charles agreed.

"Miss Florence, what about you?" asked Brock.

"I don't know either, and I have thought about who would kill my dear, sweet mother. I feel anger, rage and hurt and I want revenge, but I don't want to feel this way." Florence gave way to tears and was embraced by her sister and father.

"Please forgive my questions, we will leave it there for now, and return tomorrow morning Mr McSorley" said Brock.

"Goodnight Sirs" replied Mr McSorley.

Brock and Charles walked the short distance to the Market House.

"Charles, Millie is an attractive girl, is she not? Without a doubt we must establish if she has a male companion" stated Brock.

"Yes I agree. I will call for you in my carriage at ten o'clock tomorrow morning, if that's convenient for you Brock?" asked Charles.

"Yes Charles, thank you and sleep well" said Brock.

"You too my friend" said Charles.

"Yes, I will if I can" replied Brock as he turned to leave. His spirit brightened as he rode home again. A broad smile broke out on his face as he thought of Veronica, "I think I'm in love!" he shouted, "No I am in love!" He then realised that he had drawn attention to himself and felt somewhat embarrassed.

Upon arriving home he was greeted by Veronica and his family. He looked at his mother and father (even though he knew the means of his discovery as a baby, they were to him still his mother and father), he loved them dearly and they him. His father Bruce, a fine, handsome man who read a lot, and his mother Elizabeth, a homely, good looking woman who loved to paint and cook. Brock loved her wheaten bread, he'd never tasted any better.

Try as he may he could not help thinking about the despicable crime that had occurred in Ballymena as he enjoyed his evening meal and of course the company. Brock's father, a man who required that the proper etiquette as respects his son and Veronica be observed, had arranged for her to be driven home in the carriage at ten o'clock. Brock was allowed to bid her goodnight with a kiss and embrace.

Brock retired at ten thirty but could not sleep. "How can I learn to control my feelings" he thought, "I must, otherwise I will never be able to confront evil."

Eventually after much restlessness he did sleep.

Ned Byrne

Chapter Three

Brock awoke at six o'clock, washed and dressed and after eating rode into Ballymena, arriving about eight o'clock. Once again he tied Duke at the back of the Market House. It was a cold but sunny morning. He needed this time on his own to reflect and revisit the scene of the crime. Again he paced back and forth in Meeting House Lane, arms folded, pondering. "The clenched fist, the wounds, these are clues" he thought to himself. He also knew in his mind that the funeral this day could also produce further evidence for him, at least that is what he hoped. He strode purposely back to Duke and rode home.

Charles Kinhilt arrived punctually at ten o'clock. "Good day my friend, are you ready for the funeral?" he inquired.

"Yes Charles, the funeral will be interesting" responded Brock.

"Interesting?" Charles questioned.

"Yes interesting" Brock confirmed, "I expect to collate some further evidence today Charles. Could I ask you to pay close attention to the mourners please?" asked Brock.

"Why Brock?" asked Charles.

"Let's get in the carriage and I will explain further as we travel into Ballymena" said Brock.

"What is this all about Brock?" questioned Charles.

"Well my friend, I expect the killer will attend the funeral, perhaps because of a morbid curiosity" replied Brock.

"You say killer, not killers, how do you know Brock?" said Charles.

"Mrs McSorley was attacked by one person only" stated Brock, "and the attacker was to her front, not behind her."

"How so?" asked Charles.

"Well she had defence wounds on her hands, especially on her right hand" answered Brock.

"Defence wounds?" said Charles puzzled.

"Well when someone is attacked, they instinctively defend themselves if they are able. Mrs McSorley tried in vain to defend herself. In doing so she pulled some of the attackers hair and it remained in her closed fist, I recovered some at the scene. The attacker has reddish hair I think" said Brock.

"This is a fantastic clue" responded Charles.

"Yes my friend it is excellent evidence, but there is more. Within Mrs McSorley's hand there was also some shorter hair, jet black in colour" stated Brock.

"But you just said there was only one attacker, now you're telling me that Mrs McSorley had two types of hair in her hand" said Charles.

"Yes, but it is the same person Charles. I believe the short black hairs to be from the attackers eyebrow. Mrs McSorley, poor woman, certainly put up a good defence" said Brock grimly.

"Not good enough though" Charles replied sadly.

"No indeed, but she will still be able to help identify her killer Charles. I believe he has reddish hair and thick, black eyebrows, and judging by the blood on the victims hand and the length of her nails, he is I think badly scratched" said Brock.

Never was there seen in Ballymena so many people in attendance at a funeral. The cortege proceeded along Shambles Street turning left onto Bridge Street and proceeded past the Market House and onto the Parish Church.

Brock walked slowly through the crowd observing all the males present, young and old to see if any matched his description. Charles waited outside the church doing precisely the same thing. By ten past one the service had been completed and neither Brock nor Charles came upon any man fitting Brock's description. Needless to say both men were bitterly disappointed. They met again in Castles Street as arranged.

"Charles, can we ride in your carriage out to O'Neil's Public House in Broughshane?" asked Brock.

"Yes of course, have you someone in mind?" inquired Charles.

"Yes I wish to speak with a man who I am sure shall be in attendance at this particular venue" stated Brock.

"May I ask who?" said Charles.

Brock hesitated then said "Yes Charles, John Killane, the petty thief. I have known you for sometime now my friend, and am privileged to work with you, I know you to be a discreet man, so I will elaborate for you. During our last visit to O'Neill's bar, I left you and the landlord Thomas for some minutes."

"Yes I remember" responded Charles.

"Well I was speaking with a certain John Peter Killane, he is a felon and a thief although non violent, and he is a regular in O'Neill's and various other establishments in Ballymena as he enjoys his drink Charles. I use him from time to time to elicit information from him" said Brock.

"How is it that he assists you?" asked Charles.

"That my friend is another story" said Brock touching the side of his nose, "sufficient it is to say he is always keen to help me in my investigations. I trust he will do the same on this occasion" continued Brock.

As the men approached O'Neill's Brock caught sight of his informant Killane leaving the premises.

"John!" Brock shouted.

On seeing Brock in the carriage he approached.

"Come in John" said Brock.

John seated himself in the carriage but looked uncomfortable.

"This is my friend Charles, you may feel as free to talk in his presence as you are in mine" said Brock. "Have you news John?" he inquired.

"Sir, you asked me to look out for someone in the cobbler trade with reddish hair and thick black eyebrows?" queried John Killane.

"I did indeed, and what else did I say about that person?" asked Brock.

"You said he would be quite small maybe five foot four or five foot five inches tall" replied Killane.

"That is correct John, tell me what you have learned" stated Brock.

"Well Mr Adair, I am a thief not a murderer, and I don't like what happened to the lady, so it was easy for me to try and find out for you what I could. There is an itinerant cobbler from Glenarm his name is Ryan, John Ryan, he's about twenty five years old. Ryan wanders from village to village repairing shoes, all his money goes on drink and he gets angry quick. I do not know where he was on the night of the Ballymena murder but I do know he had been seen here in Broughshane on market day. That market day had many stalls dealing with footwear" said Killane.

"Yes John it did" said Brock, "I'm obliged to you" and pressing some coins into Killane's hand Brock said "get yourself a drink, no doubt we'll speak again."

"Yes sir I'm sure we will Mr Adair sir" said Killane walking away.

Looking pensive now Brock muttered "why, why would this fellow Ryan attack Mrs McSorley. There must be a reason. Can we return to Shambles Street Charles, I must speak with the McSorley's, it is of some urgency?" asked Brock.

The carriage sped towards Ballymena; Brock sat arms folded, many mutterings coming from his mouth. The carriage stopped outside the family home on Shambles Street.

"May we come in Mr McSorley, and please accept our apologies for disturbing you on this day" said Brock.

"That is alright Mr Adair, Mr Kinhilt" said Mr McSorley, who was looking somewhat more pale and thin since the last time they had spoke.

"Sir I have some more information, but I need to ask you and your daughters some questions urgently, may I?" asked Brock.

"Yes, yes of course, Florence and Millie!" he shouted, "please come here."

Both sisters arrived together, needless to say both looked weak and drawn. Both Brock and Charles felt great compassion for them.

"I fear I should have asked this question sooner, but nonetheless I will ask it now" said Brock. "Do any of you know a red haired man in his twenties, quite small in height?"

Florence interrupted "I know two or three people of that description, both are farm hands, one in Galgorm and one in Cullybackey, but that is all."

"Mr McSorley?" asked Charles.

"No, I do not know anyone of that description" replied Mr McSorley.

"Thank you for your time then" sighed Brock. Just as Brock and Charles were about to leave Millie shouted "the other day mother answered the door to a man like that, red hair!"

Mr McSorley cradled his daughter, "tell us more Mille, tell Mr Adair and Mr Kinhilt."

"Dad" Millie was sobbing now, "the other day a man called and spoke with mammy at the door, he was talking funny. He was talking about fixing shoes, cheap like."

"What did your mother say" asked her father.

"Mammy told him that she didn't need any shoes mended" replied Millie.

"Millie" said Brock quietly "you said he was talking funny, what do you mean?"

"I think he was not able to speak properly, he was very hard to understand. He was angry as well. I couldn't hear everything that was said but mammy told him to go away. She shut the door and I remember her saying something like "that silly man" stated Millie.

"Thank you Millie" said Brock, "we will not bother you again. Mr McSorley, Florence and Millie, we will leave you in peace."

"Please get the person who did this Mr Adair, please get him" pleaded Mr McSorley.

"We will do our best sir, we will speak again" replied Brock, "goodbye."

Brock and Charles made their way to the carriage.

"Do you think this is the same man?" asked Charles.

"It is a strong possibility Charles, let us go to Captain Dickey and inform him of our findings" said Brock.

A short time later they met with Captain Dickey.

"Gentlemen, good to see you both, you have good news?" asked the Captain.

"Yes, and no Captain" said Brock. Brock outlined the result of his investigation to date, including the suspects name – John Ryan of Glenarm.

"We need to arrest him, I will have a military detachment scour the area, but where do we start?" asked the Captain.

"May I suggest something?" said Charles. "May I suggest that a seach is made of the highway that goes from Ballymena to Glenarm, especially the bars."

"It is a good idea, we shall start there" said the Captain.

"I must speak to the cobbler in Church Street, Mr McArthur. Let us go there Charles, goodbye Captain, we shall be in touch" said Brock.

Brock walked with Charles to Church Street, the conversation was little, both men had deep thoughts in respects to the killer.

"Gentlemen" said Mr McArthur, "your boots are ready sir, new leather soles and heels with metal clips as instructed."

Brock examine the boots, "excellent work Mr McArthur."

"You will get miles of use from those boots" said Mr McArthur.

"Yes and I shall enjoy polishing them" said Brock.

"I noticed that your boots were well tended to, a thick layer of polish, not too thick though. May I ask sir, were you in the military at any time?" inquired the cobbler.

"No" said Brock laughing, "but I have watched many a soldier polish his boots, and I've followed suit. It has a calming effect on me. Mr McArthur, do you know an itinerant cobbler called,"

"Ryan!" interrupted Mr McArthur, "you mean John Ryan, from Carnlough, no Glenarm. He is an unstable young man."

"How do you mean?" asked Charles.

"Well he is prone to fits of anger when he fails to get his way. He has asked me in the past for employment but I would not, indeed I could not employ him. He would frighten my customers, he frightens me" said Mr McArthur.

"What does he look like?" asked Charles.

"He is about five foot four or so, he has striking red hair and strange black eyebrows, very black" replied Mr McArthur.

"When did you last see him?" asked Charles.

Mr McArthur rubbed his chin and thought for a moment, then replied "I think it was last week, yes, last week. He was walking along Shambles Street."

"Is there anything else about this man that might interest us?" asked Brock.

"I cannot think of anything, but if I do I will let you know" replied the cobbler.

"Thank you Mr McArthur, we will no doubt speak again" said Brock.

Brock and Charles left the premises having paid for the boots. As both men walked along Church Street, Brock felt a sense of anticipation and excitement, yet he felt guilty that someone had lost their life. Someone had lost a mother, a wife, a daughter, the list went on he thought, and here he was feeling excitement. Again he told himself if he was to continue as a investigator he must try and remain neutral in his emotion.

Charles and Brock continued along Church Street and just as they reached the Market House one of Captain Dickey's men rode up quickly.

"Mr Adair sir, Captain Dickey requires you immediately at his quarters" stated the soldier.

"Thank you, tell him we will be with him forthwith" answered Brock. "Never mind the carriage Charles, let us run to the Captain's quarters, I do think this is going to be of the utmost importance."

"What is it Captain?" inquired Brock as he entered the quarters.

"We have arrested Ryan. My men apprehended him en route to Broughshane, he was still in Ballymena" said the Captain.

"Your men should feel proud Captain" said Brock still slightly out of breath from the run.

"You may speak with Ryan now if you wish" said the Captain.

"Yes let us establish the facts now" said Brock.

"I think we should calm ourselves first" said Charles.

"A good idea" agreed Captain Dickey.

"Yes I concur" said Brock, "can we have some tea?"

"Yes of course" said Captain Dickey.

After enjoying their tea Brock said "it will be good to conclude this case, I hope he is our man."

"Bring the prisoner in here" ordered Captain Dickey.

Two soldiers stood either side of the prisoner.

"This, Ryan, is Mr Brock Adair and his companion Mr Charles Kinhilt, they wish to speak with you about a matter" said Captain Dickey.

"I know I'm not guilty of killing that woman" stated Ryan.

"You know then why you have been arrested?" asked Brock.

"You fit the description of the killer" said Charles.

"So what" snarled Ryan.

"You know why you have been arrested" asked Brock again.

"For the murder of Mrs McSorley" said Ryan.

"You can tell us where you were on Thursday night past?" asked Brock.

"Yeah, I was with my brother at home in Glenarm" stated Ryan.

"Your home, where in Glenarm?" asked Brock.

"The Vennel" said Ryan.

"Who else will vouch for your whereabouts?" inquired Brock.

"Just my brother, Ned" Ryan replied.

"You have a brother called Ned?" asked Brock.

"That's what I just said" snarled Ryan again.

"You are going to be detained here until we verify your alibi" said Brock.

All three men left Ryan. "Well, what do you think?" asked Captain Dickey.

"Captain, I wish to speak urgently with the prisoners brother Ned, from the Vennel in Glenarm" Brock said.

"Brock I have a contingent of men in Glenarm, I will send a rider to bring this person here if he is in attendance at home, he will be brought directly to me in the morning or by midday at least" said Captain Dickey.

"I shall be in attendance with you then Captain at one o'clock tomorrow. Excuse me now for it has been a long day and I am tired" Brock said wearily.

"That makes two of us" agreed Charles.

As Brock and Charles walked to their carriage, Charles couldn't help but ask himself anxiously, "Is it him?" He then asked Brock, "Is it him, is Ryan the killer?"

"I truly believe so" stated Brock.

As they travelled back to Brock's home near Galgorm, Brock voiced his reasons for his belief that Ryan was the killer. They were simply stated by Brock.

"Point one - his trade, he is a cobbler of sorts and I found slithers of shoe leather at the scene. Point two – his description, the red hair and striking black eyebrows, both types of hair were found in the victims fist. Point three – his height, the victim was a tall woman, yet the deep incision on her neck was at an angle, higher at the back and lower at the front, leaving no doubt that the killer was smaller than Mrs McSorley" he explained. "Yes" said Brock, "he is our man."

"Charles would you mind collecting me tomorrow about twelve noon, you are free I trust?" Brock asked.

"Yes Brock, I have no court duties until next week. I shall be glad to bring you to Ballymena, I wish to know if you can conclude this case. So goodnight my friend" said Charles warmly.

"Goodnight to you to Charles, safe journey to Crebilly" responded Brock.

Brock retired to his bed that night exhausted, but content in the knowledge that he had the killer.

Ned Byrne

Chapter Four

Brock slept well and upon waking at eight o'clock determined with ever great vigour to solve the case. He shaved and dressed hastily in his finest black suit. He wore his newly repaired boots which were handsomely polished. After a light breakfast he strolled for an hour around the garden, visiting his trusty horse Duke.

Charles arrived punctually as usual, at twelve noon.

"We shall solve this crime Charles, today I hope" declared Brock as he ran to the carriage.

"I do hope so" said Charles, "Ryan does seem confident that his brother will alibi him."

"Indeed" said Brock, "but let us see. Hopefully Captain Dickey's men will have detained him at The Vennel in Glenarm and have brought him to Ballymena."

Upon arriving at the barracks that indeed prove to be the case.

"Good morning Captain, have you been successful?" asked Brock.

"Yes gentlemen, good morning to you too. Ned Ryan awaits, although he is saying nothing to us, he is in the next room. Are you ready to speak with him?" asked Captain Dickey.

"Yes Captain" said Charles eagerly.

Captain Dickey looked disappointed, this prompted Brock to ask "Captain you look unhappy, pray tell me what is concerning you?"

"My dear friend Brock, I fear you are how shall I say it, wrong in your conclusions perhaps" said Captain Dickey glumly.

"How so sir?" asked Brock.

"You will see when you enter" replied the Captain. "Men, let Mr Adair and Mr Kinhilt speak with Ned Ryan" commanded Captain Dickey.

Brock was the first to enter the room, followed by Charles. On seeing Ned Ryan Brock and Charles simultaneously looked at each other in disbelief, for standing before them was Ned Ryan flanked by two soldiers. Also present was the suspect John Ryan again accompanied by two soldiers. The Ryan brothers were identical twins. They were the same height, with that striking red hair and thick black eyebrows. Brock felt dejected, "which is the guilty one" he thought to himself. Both brothers had facial scratches.

Brock composed himself then he said, "My name is Brock Adair, this is my colleague Mr Charles Kinhilt and we are assisting with the investigation of the murder of Mrs Florence McSorley in Meeting House Lane on Thursday evening past. Ned how did you get those cuts on your face?"

"I fell" replied Ned.

"When and where" asked Charles.

"On the rocks in the graveyard in Glenarm a couple of days ago" replied Ned.

"Strange that your brother has similar marks on his face" said Brock.

"I fell as well" said John Ryan

"How strange, how very strange" replied Brock. "Captain Dickey may I have a word outside" asked Brock. Both men left the room.

"I'm sorry Brock, now you see why I was disappointed, identical twins in every detail" said Captain Dickey.

"Yes I was shocked at first, but I will still prove which one is guilty Captain. Can you ask your men to bring young Millie McSorley here. I want to see if she can recognise who called at her house and spoke to her mother" said Brock.

"Will that help now Brock?" asked Captain Dickey.

"It will Captain, it will. Please don't let them see her" said Brock as he returned to the prisoners.

"I am convinced one of you is the murderer of Mrs McSorley, and I shall prove it. What is your occupation Ned?" asked Brock.

"I'm a thatcher, and a good one" replied Ned.

"So you are skilled with cutting tools" said Brock.

"I certainly am" replied Ned.

"John, you are a cobbler, also skilled with a knife" stated Brock.

"Yes of course, no great discovery there then" snapped John. Both brothers laughed.

The suspect John Ryan sarcastically asked "Which one of us was it then Mr Adair? You cannot prove a thing. Let us both go, now."

Brock felt his anger swell up. "Perhaps you should both go, to the gallows" he said, only to get a disapproving look from Charles, a look that only a lawyer can give.

At that point Captain Dickey entered the room. "May I have a word Brock."

Out of earshot of the Ryan brothers the Captain informed Brock that Millie had arrived.

"Please have her pass by the room, tell her to look at the Ryan brothers as she passes and I will speak with her.

"That will be done" said Captain Dickey.

Brock returned to the room, arms folded. "Why" he asked loudly, "would the innocent twin protect the guilty one? Is he frightened, is he less manly than his brother? Will the guilty one be content if the innocent one is sent to the gallows gentlemen, and I use that word in the loosest sense. What is it to be?"

"Prove it Adair, we are innocent, not guilty, let us go" replied both brothers.

Captain Dickey entered the room. "I need to speak with you Brock" said the Captain.

"What did Millie say?" asked Brock

"She is here" responded the Captain.

"Hello Millie, I know this is difficult for you. Did you see the two men?" asked Brock.

"They are both the same" said Millie, "I do not know which one spoke to Mammy, but it was one of them I'm sure, really sure."

"Millie thank you, you are a brave young lady and I will speak to your father and sister soon" said Brock. He returned to the room.

"John, Ned, can you write?" asked Brock.

"I can" said Ned.

"So can I" shouted John. "Do you think we are uneducated, our mother taught us to write."

"Please bring a quill and ink" requested Brock.

Ned Ryan was the first to sign his name. John Ryan did likewise. To the astonishment of Brock on examining their signatures he noted that both men had fine writing. "Captain Dickey, you may charge John Ryan with the murder of Mrs Florence McSorley" stated Brock.

Captain Dickey with a worried look on his face requested Brock to come outside, then he asked Brock, "Why are you so sure John Ryan is the murderer. Please give me the facts before we charge him with murder. We do not have any admission of guilt, the suspects are identical twins and there are no witnesses" said the Captain annoyed.

"Captain Dickey sir, please let us return to the room to prove John Ryan's guilt to you and Charles, and of course later to the court" said Brock.

Brock and the Captain entered the room. "Proceed" requested the Captain.

"Thank you" said Brock, he continued, "although you are both identical twins, I will outline my reasons proving beyond doubt that you John Ryan are the murderer. You had an argument with Mrs McSorley at her home the other day, on Thursday."

"So did I!" shouted Ned.

"Be quiet!" commanded Captain Dickey. "Continue Brock."

"You followed her to her mothers and waited until she returned home in the dark, and you attacked her in Meeting House Lane. The victim was five foot eleven and you are five foot four inches tall. You confronted her, no doubt mentioning your call at her home, and in an obvious frenzy you produce your sharp cobblers knife. You cut her neck and because you are smaller than her, this was higher at the back of her neck and lower as it cut to the front of her neck. This is consistent with an attack from the front by a smaller person.

You also stabbed her about twelve times down the side of her body. Your knife and no doubt your pocket contained, understandably, given your trade, slithers of leather which I also found with the body.

Mrs McSorley had in her right hand which was clenched, red hair and shorter black hair from your eyebrows. She had long nails, three of them contained blood and hair showing she had tried to defend herself. The killer, therefore, should have marks on his face, at least three. John Ryan has such marks."

"But so does Ned Ryan" said Captain Dickey.

"That is correct Captain. However," Brock continued, "Ned Ryan's marks are only on his cheek, his eyebrows seem intact. John Ryan's marks extend from his forehead to the lower cheek. Finally, Ned Ryan is right handed and John Ryan is left handed as was demonstrated when they wrote their signatures. The killer is left handed."

John and Ned Ryan gave each other a worried look.

Brock carried on. "The wounds, all of them, were on the right hand side of the victim, inflicted by someone left handed. Mrs McSorley being right handed, scratched her attacker on the left hand side of his face as he faced her. John Ryan's wounds are on the left side of his face whereas Ned's are on the right hand side. Ned's scratches were inflicted by his left handed brother. Have you anything to say?" Brock directed the question at both men. Neither man replied. "Ned you will doubtless spend a long time in prison, maybe even in a far away place."

Ned began to move away slowly from his brother John, this movement was noticed by all present including John who gave him a menacing look.

"I want to speak to Mr Adair, alone" shouted Ned.

"Don't you open your mouth!" screamed John "or I will" - He did not finish the sentence, but it was clear to all what his intent was.

Captain Dickey then turned to John Ryan and said "You will today be charged with the murder of Mrs Florence McSorley". The captain then ordered his soldiers to escort John Ryan to his cell leaving only Ned in the room. "Speak now with Mr Adair and Mr Kinhilt Ned and tell them what you have to say" urged Captain Dickey.

Ned was shaking by now and needed a glass of water, having drained the glass of it's contents he said, "John came home on Friday afternoon, he had stolen a horse in Ballymena and rode it hard home. I knew he was in trouble the moment I saw him. He was freshly cut down his face, he threw his knife in the water butt outside our back door. He told me he had been in a fight in Ballymena and he asked me to say that he was with me all Thursday. He said that the military were looking for him. I have always been scared of him, he's a bully, he said that he would do something to me and that it would hurt. I didn't get a chance to ask what, he just suddenly scratched me really hard on the face. He didn't say why he did it, but he did say he would kill me if I didn't say I was with him all Thursday. I know some of his friends, Thomas Archer is one of them, he a highwayman with a posse, and I am really frightened of him."

"Yes a dangerous felon." Murmured Brock he waited as Ned continued.

"I'm sorry that I lied but I was scared. He knows that I have a girlfriend in Glenarm, her name is Sally and she lives in Toberwine Street. She's unable to walk properly and people laugh at her, but I like her a lot and she likes me. John said he would kill her before he killed me, so you see I had to lie to you. Will he be kept a prisoner Mr Adair?"

"I think so Ned, I think so" replied Brock, "What do you say Charles?"

"I would agree with Mr Adair, Ned, and with Captain Dickey's permission I would respectfully suggest that the court be told that you assisted with this enquiry."

"I concur" said Captain Dickey.

"You will be kept here until our enquiries are complete" said Brock. "Captain Dickey could your men check that water barrel for that knife just as a means of supporting what Ned has said?"

"Of course Brock" stated Captain Dickey.

"I will inform Mr McSorley and his daughters of the result of our enquiry today Captain, and I shall with Charles attend the court hearing in due course" said Brock.

As they left the barracks Captain Dickey said "I wish to thank you and Charles for your assistance and I shall look forward to dining with you both soon" said Captain Dickey warmly.

"Thank you Captain and I shall bring Veronica. Charles though has no-one yet to bring" Brock said jokingly.

"You would be surprised" said Charles, "I am a good looking man waiting for the right lady!"

"Indeed you are" said Captain Dickey in an amused tone, "I look forward to our meal, good day gentlemen."

"Good day Captain" both men replied in unison.

Having informed Mr McSorley and his daughters of the result of the enquiry, Brock and Charles walked the short distance to the Market House to collect the horses.

"I am going home to play my new musical instrument Charles, and one day I shall play for your enjoyment, perhaps at your wedding" teased Brock.

"What is this instrument?" enquired Charles.

"It is a harp, and a fine one it is too" replied Brock.

"Goodness no, a harp played by you, I'm glad you live a good distance from me Brock, anyway how will you be able to master it?" asked Charles.

"How do you mean Charles" asked Brock.

"Well I've never heard of a left handed harpist" replied Charles.

"You will" said Brock, "you will."

"I bid you good day my friend" said Brock.

"I shall see you soon" replied Charles as both men rode to their homes.

Ned Ryan was not charged with any offences. His brother John Ryan was found guilty by the Court of Assizes and sentenced to death. He was hanged at Ballymena Moat at six o'clock in the morning on Friday 16th December 1796. The hanging was witnessed by Captain Dickey, Brock Adair, Charles Kinhilt and a large crowd. His body was left hanging for one day and buried without a marker in Ballymena. Mr McSorley, Florence and Millie continue to live in Shambles Street and have been well supported by the community.

John Ryan's cobblers' knife was indeed found in the water butt in Glenarm.

Incidentally the horse used in the hanging of John Ryan was called Millie.